This special edition was printed for Kohl's Department Stores, Inc. (for distribution on behalf of Kohl's Cares,
LLC, its wholly owned subsidiary), by Disney Press, New York/Los Angeles.

Kohl's
1224425-00
123387
09/14–10/14

Printed in China
First Edition
1 3 5 7 9 10 8 6 4 2
ISBN 978-1-4847-2382-1 • G615-7693-2-14286

For more Disney Press fun, visit www.disneybooks.com

DISNEP PRESS
New York • Los Angeles

Nemo was a little clownfish. He lived a quiet life with his dad, Marlin, on the Great Barrier Reef. Nemo longed for adventure. But Marlin worried about the dangers of the ocean. He barely let Nemo out of his sight.

On the first day of school, Marlin overheard Nemo and his
friends daring each other to swim out over a steep cliff.
icked. "Nemo, you know you can't swim well!"

ad," Nemo said.

boat on the surface.

red behind him.

● ● ● ● ● ●

The diver pulled out a net and caught Nemo. Then he took Nemo back to his boat. As he sped off, he accidentally knocked a diving mask overboard.

Marlin chased after the boat, but it was too fast. Marlin wasn't ready to give up. "Has anybody seen a boat?" he asked any fish who would listen.

Just then, Marlin bumped into a fish named Dory.

"Hey, I've seen a boat!" she said. "Follow me!" But Dory suffered from short-term memory loss. As soon as they started swimming, she whirled around. "Stop following me!" she shouted.

Figuring Dory couldn't help him, Marlin turned to leave and found himself face-to-face with a shark!

The shark invited Dory and Marlin to a "party" in an old
sunken ship.

Inside were two other sharks. Together they pledged: "I am
a nice shark. Fish are friends, not food."

Suddenly, Marlin saw the diver's mask! Dory noticed
some writing on the strap. The two fish quickly left the party
carrying the mask.

Miles away, Nemo was in a fish tank at a dentist's office. The other fish and their pelican friend, Nigel, passed the time by watching the dentist work.

Nemo learned he would be given to Darla, the dentist's niece. The fish warned him that Darla's pet fish never lived for very long.

The Tank Gang's leader, Gill, took charge. He explained that if someone could jam the water filter, the dentist would take the fish out of the tank to clean it. When he put the fish in plastic bags, they could escape by rolling out the window and into the harbor.

Deep in the ocean, Dory and Marlin were in a dark canyon. Marlin struggled to hold on to the lighted antenna of an anglerfish so that Dory could study the writing on the mask.

"'P. Sherman, 42 Wallaby Way, Sydney,'" Dory read.

Marlin knew that must be the diver's address!

Marlin and Dory headed for Sydney. Suddenly, Dory bumped into a teeny tiny jellyfish. "I shall call him Squishy, and he shall be mine," she said happily.

But Squishy wasn't alone. Soon they were surrounded by an entire forest of deadly jellyfish. The jellyfish stung Dory and Marlin, making them feel weak and tired.

When Marlin woke up, he was lying on a sea turtle's shell. "Dude! Name's Crush," the turtle said, introducing himself.

Around them, hundreds of sea turtles rode with a lightning-fast current. Crush's son, Squirt, was playing with Dory. While they played, Marlin told Squirt about his search for Nemo.

Dory had already forgotten the story. "This is gonna be good. I can tell!" she said excitedly.

Squirt told the story to a lobster and the lobster told a dolphin. Soon the news spread all the way to Sydney, where Nigel the pelican heard it.

Nigel sped off to the dentist's office. "Your dad's been fighting the entire ocean looking for you," he told Nemo. "And the word is, he's headed this way right now—to Sydney!"

"Really?" Nemo asked. He couldn't believe his dad was so adventurous! Nemo realized that if he was ever going to get home, he had to be brave, too. He took a deep breath and carefully jammed a pebble into the tank's filter, stopping its swirling blades. Soon the tank would be so dirty the dentist would have to clean it.

In the morning, the tank was still clean! Nemo's escape plan was ruined!

Just then, the dentist captured Nemo in a plastic bag. As he lifted Nemo out of the tank, the office door slammed open. Darla had arrived. The dentist looked at the plastic bag. Inside, Nemo was floating belly up. Nemo winked at his friends. He was pretending to be dead.

Outside Sydney, Marlin and Dory had met Nigel, who flew them straight to the dentist's office. The pelican soared inside with the two fish in his beak.

Marlin saw Nemo floating upside down in the bag. "Nemo!" he cried. He thought his son was dead.

The dentist shooed Nigel away. "Out with ya. And stay out!"

Nigel returned to the harbor and dropped Marlin and Dory into the water. Marlin swam out to sea, leaving Dory. "We were too late," he said.

But after Marlin left, Nemo swam out of a nearby pipe. He had been flushed! Nemo spotted Dory swimming in circles.

"Are you all right?" he asked. "I'm Nemo."

"You're Nemo!" Dory cried, hugging him happily.

Nemo and Dory found Marlin nearby.

"Daddy!" Nemo called out.

Marlin was so happy to see his son. But as they swam
toward each other, a big net dropped into the water. Dory
got stuck inside.

Nemo knew just what to do. "Tell all the fish to swim
down!" Together, the fish swam down until the net broke.

Marlin found Nemo pinned beneath the heavy net. To his enormous relief, his son's eyes fluttered open. Nemo was going to be all right!

Marlin finally realized that even though Nemo was a little fish, he was capable of doing very big things! It was time for Nemo, Marlin, and Dory to go home.

Several weeks later, Nemo was back home and ready for school. This time, Marlin was ready, too. He knew that his son could take care of himself.

Nemo waved as he swam away. "Bye, Dad. Oh, wait! I forgot something!" He swam back and hugged Marlin. "Love you, Dad."

Marlin smiled. "I love you, too, son," he said. "Now, go have an adventure!"